TOO LOUD LILY

To Gail – S. L.

Library of Congress Cataloging-in-Publication Data Available

ISBN 0-439-57913-9

10 9 8 7 6 5 4 3 2 1   04 05 06 07 08
Printed in China

The display text was set in Coop Black.
The text type was set in L VAG Rounded Light.
Book design by Yvette Awad

First American edition, March 2004

BY
SOFIE
LAGUNA
ILLUSTRATED
BY
KERRY
ARGENT

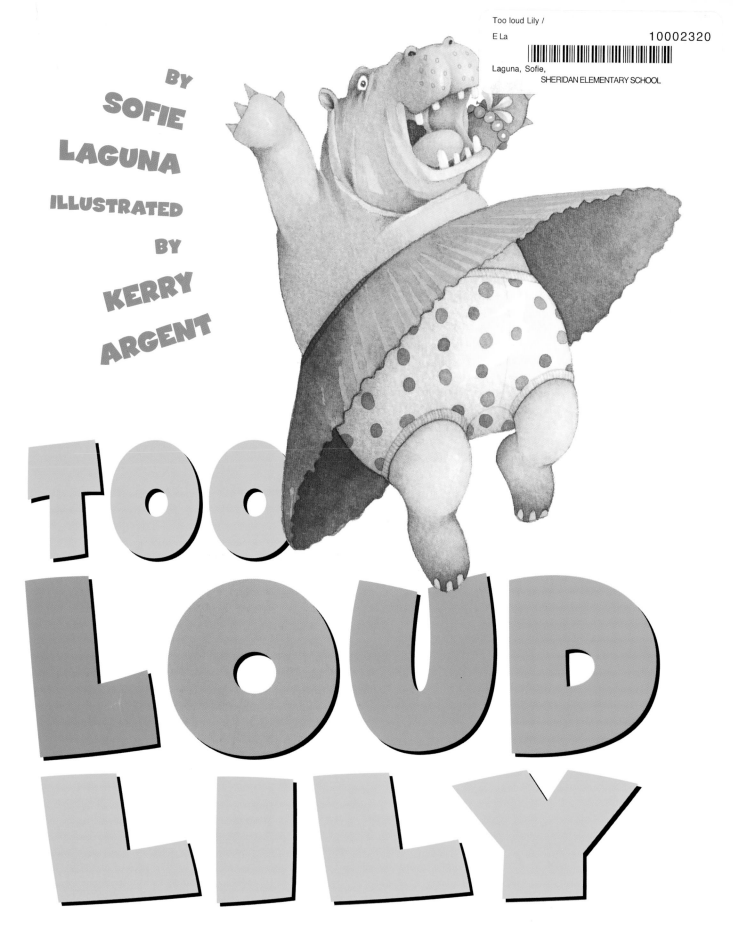

TOO LOUD LILY

Scholastic Press • New York

Everyone told Lily Hippo she was too loud.

"Lily Hippo, keep it down please – I can't hear myself think!" said Dad.

"Lily Hippo, sing quietly – you'll wake the baby!" said Mom.

"Lily Hippo, you make more noise than a herd of wild elephants!" said Lily's big brother.

Lily tried doing something very quiet. . . .

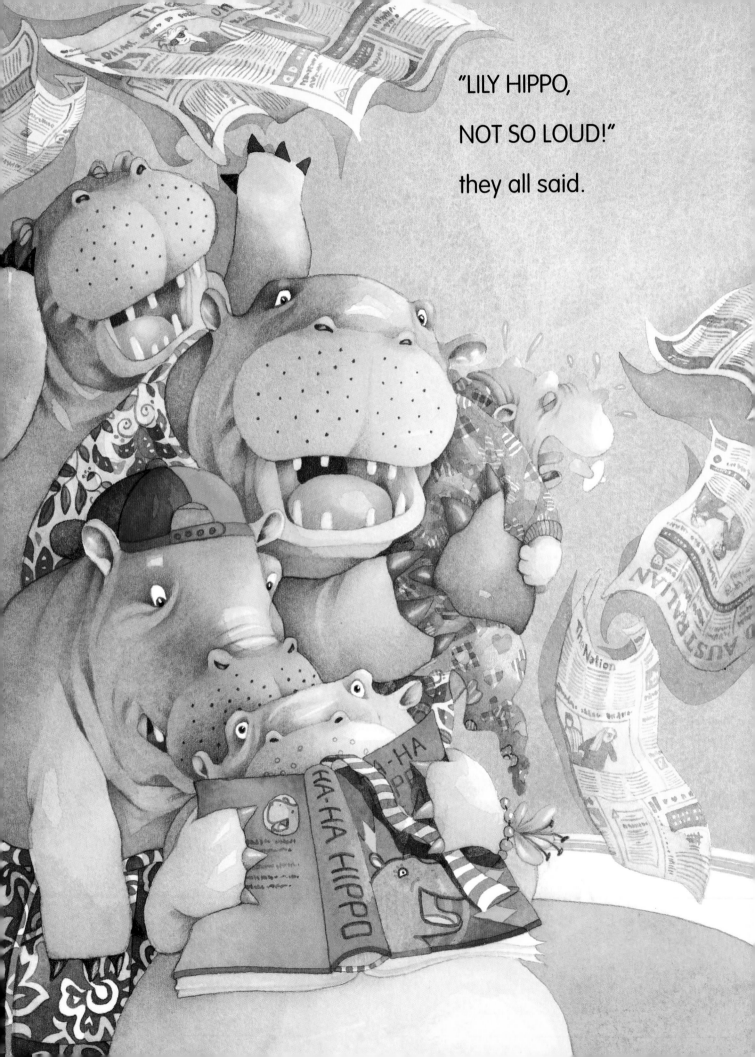

"LILY HIPPO,

NOT SO LOUD!"

they all said.

At school, Lily's best friends were Hester and Lou.

Sometimes even Hester and Lou
were upset with Lily.

She was too loud.

Then a new teacher came to Lily's school.
Her name was Miss Loopiola, and she wore
a big red poncho. She taught music and drama.

Lily liked Miss Loopiola. She decided to be in the
school play.

On the first day of rehearsals, Miss Loopiola taught everyone a fast-stomping dance.

Lily tried to do the dance very quietly.

"Wonderful work!" called out Miss Loopiola.
"But you could try stomping just a little louder
this time, please!"

Lily *really* liked Miss Loopiola.

Lily stomped a lot louder.

"Magnificent!" cried Miss Loopiola.

"Lily Hippo, would you like to lead the dance?"

Lily *loved* Miss Loopiola.

Lily was in charge of crashing the cymbals and banging the drums for storm noises, . . .

growling and roaring for the fierce lion noises, . . .

cackling and screeching for the wicked witch noises, . . .

singing the song about the very brave prince, . . .

and clapping in time to
all the music.

On the night of the play, Lily was very nervous.

What if she forgot what to do?

What if she tried to speak and no words came out?

Or even worse – what if she was too loud?

Lily could feel her heart thumping and her
knees shaking.

The room was very, very quiet.

Everybody was waiting for Lily.
"Go on Lily," whispered Miss Loopiola.

"Nice and LOUD!"

Lily took a deep breath.

"Let the show begin!"

she said in her loudest stage voice.

Lily did her best fast-
stomping, . . .

her best crashing and banging, . . .

her best growling and roaring, . . .

her best cackling and screeching, . . .

and her best singing and clapping.

And everybody loved it.

"Hooray for Lily Hippo!"
they cried out.

The sound of all that clapping

and stamping and cheering was

very special and very, very

loud – a bit like Lily.

- big, loud
  hippo finds
  her niche
- differences/strengths